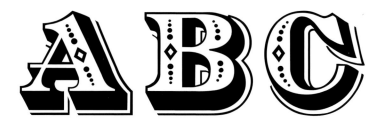

ABC

A Child's First Alphabet Book

ALISON JAY

Dutton Children's Books
New York

Aa   **a** is for **apple**

Bb   b is for **balloon**

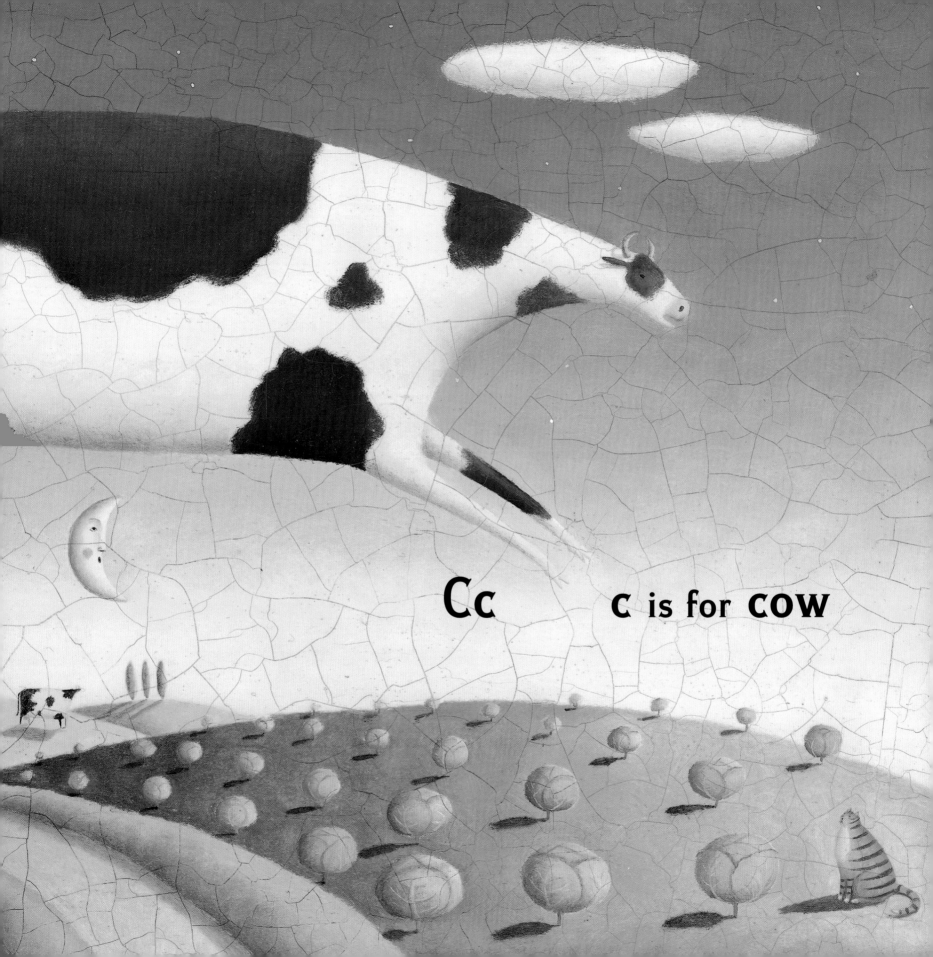

Cc   c is for **COW**

Dd   **d** is for **dog**

Ee   **e** is for **elephant**

Ff f is for **frog**

Gg g is for giraffe

Hh   h is for **horse**

li   i is for **ice cream**

Jj

j is for **jack-in-the-box**

Kk   k is for **keyhole**

Ll   **l** is for **lion**

Mm m is for moon

Nn   n is for **nest**

Oo   o is for **owl**

Pp   p is for **panda**

Qq   q is for **quilt**

Rr   r is for rabbit

Ss   s is for **shell**

Tt   t is for **treasure chest**

Uu   u is for **unicorn**

Vv   v is for **vase**

Ww

w is for whale

Xx   X marks the **spot!**

Yy   y is for **yacht**

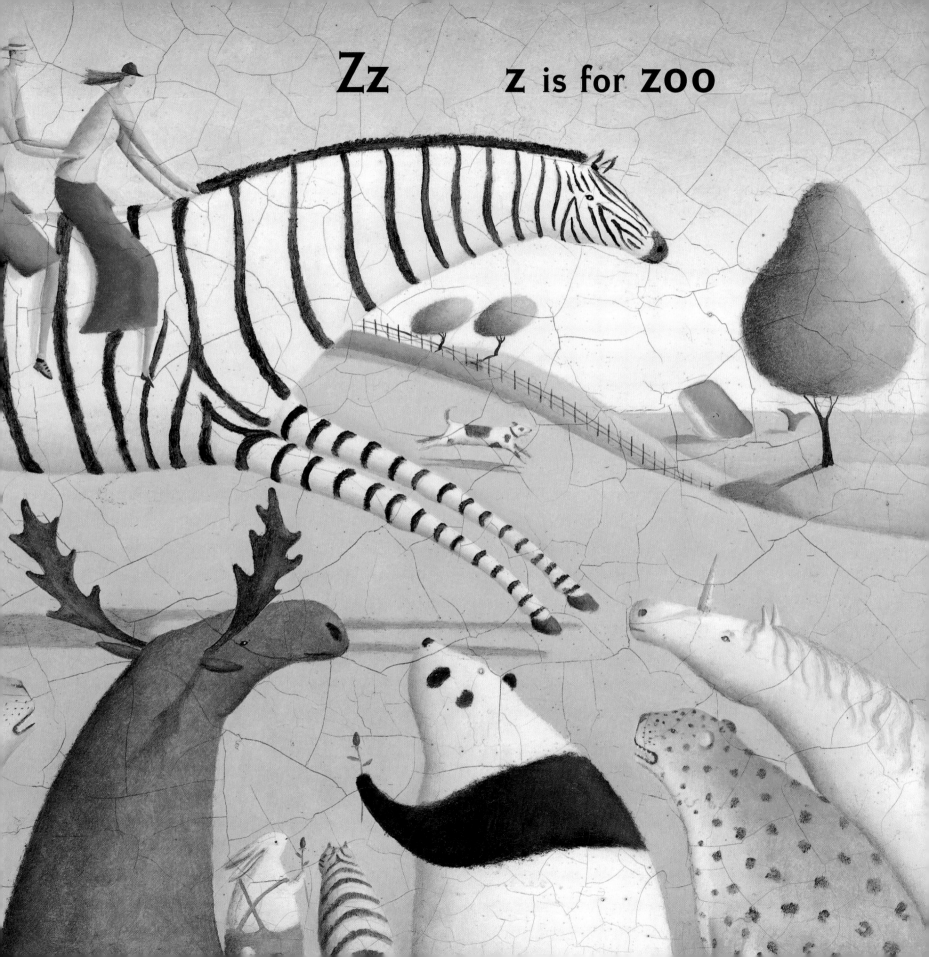

Zz   z is for **ZOO**

Aa
airplane
ant
apple
artist

Bb
ball
balloon
basket
bee
beehive
bucket
butterfly

Cc
cabbage
car
cat
chicken
cow

Dd
daisy
diamond
dog
doll
door
doughnut
duck

Ee
elephant
envelope
explorer

Ff
fish
fishing pole
flower
fly
frog

Gg
garden
gate
giraffe
glasses
goose

Hh
hat
heart
horse
horseshoe
house

Ii
ice cream
iguana
insects
island

Jj
jack-in-the-box
Jell-O
jug

Kk
kangaroo
key
keyhole
koala

Ll
ladder
ladybug
lemon
lion

Mm
map
moon
moose
mountain

Nn
nest
night

Oo
owl

Pp
panda
peach
pear
pepper
picnic
pie
postcard
pumpkin

Qq
quail
queen
question mark
quilt

Rr
rabbit
rain
rainbow
rose
rowboat

Ss
sandcastle
sea
seaweed
shell
ship
shoe
shovel
starfish

Tt
treasure
treasure chest
trumpet

Uu
umbrella

unicorn
upside down

Vv
vase
violets
violin

Ww
wave
whale
windmill

Xx
X marks the spot!

Yy
yacht

Zz
zebra
zoo

For Diana and Ian

Illustrations copyright © 2003 by Alison Jay
Text copyright © 2003 by The Templar Company plc
All rights reserved.
CIP Data is available.

Published in the United States 2003 by Dutton Children's Books,
a division of Penguin Young Readers Group
345 Hudson Street, New York, New York 10014
www.penguinputnam.com

First published in the UK 2003 by Templar Publishing,
an imprint of The Templar Company plc, Surrey

Concept by Dugald Steer

Printed in Belgium
First American Edition
ISBN 0-525-46951-6
1 3 5 7 9 10 8 6 4 2